Dear Sue —
    Just to remind you
that you are always near
        with love
        Nancy

MOONLIGHT MEMOIRS

Remembering that Family and Friends are Forever

Maggie Mei Lewis

Illustrated by Melody Lea Lamb

Publisher's Cataloging-in-Publication (Provided by Quality Books, Inc.)
Lewis, Maggie Mei.
Moonlight memoirs : remembering that family and friends are forever / Maggie Mei Lewis ; illustrated by Melody Lea Lamb. -- 1st ed.   p. cm.
SUMMARY: One moonlit winter's night, two young mice follow an older mouse who, along with several other animal friends, teaches them a comforting life lesson.
ISBN-13: 978-0-578-01415-9
ISBN-10: 0-578-01415-7
1. Loss (Psychology)--Religious aspects—Juvenile fiction. 2. Future life--Juvenile fiction. 3. Mice--Juvenile fiction. [1. Loss (Psychology)--Fiction. 2. Future life--Fiction. 3. Mice--Fiction.]
I. Lamb, Melody Lea, ill. II. Title.
PZ7.L587265Moo 2009   [Fic]
QBI09-600071
Juvenile fiction.

Printed in the United States of America
First Edition
Editors: Carolyn Madison and Shawn Mahshie
Book Design: Jonathan Gullery

Published by:

GOOD TIMES PRESS, LLC.
Edgewater, Maryland 21037
www.goodtimespress.com

To my whole family, my loving pets, my amazing friends
and everyone who has helped me throughout my life.

To Jennifer Hua Tam, my best buddy since our childhood in China.

To Leah Canale, who reminded me why I wanted to write this book.

To Luke Senior and Luke Junior, two extraordinary cowboys.

And to my grandma, who brought flowers into the world.

Maggie Mei Lewis

Two mice - one black and one white
Follow each other on a cold, lonely night.

What are they up to?
Where are they going?
They hurry through shadows
Under the moon's silent glowing.

An old silver mouse
Kindly gives them a nod,
Then waits for them to follow.

How odd.

He leads them into the darkening night,
The moon slowly slips out of sight.
Tiny paws trample through the icy snow.
They follow the silver mouse, heads hanging low.

Where will he take them?   What's the occasion?

Snowflakes fall as their new silver friend
Guides them around yet another bend.

"Why am I here?" the white mouse questions.
"You are here," replies the silver mouse,
"To learn a great lesson."

"We're almost there, so let's keep on going.
It looks as if it's started snowing."

Little paws prance
As snowflakes dance,
And sometimes they pause
For just a quick glance.

Finally they stop at a snow-covered clearing
Where curious things begin appearing.
Creatures emerge–out of nowhere, it seems!
Both mice wonder, "Am I in a dream?"

The animals glow
With a soft gentle light,
So the young mice know
Everything is alright.

A silver-white rabbit speaks to the mice,
Smiling a kind small smile.
"Although you might not know us,
We've been with you awhile."

The sky above clears as it stops snowing,
While all around the animals are glowing.
Then the old silver mouse and a pale tabby cat
Begin to talk in a strange sort of chat.

After a while, when their chat is all done,
The brightness fades as darkness comes.
One by one, the animals grow quiet,
And then the whole clearing is finally silent.

The two mice sit there, just looking around.
Until from the great sky, something softly floats down.

Then all of a sudden they both clearly see–
"A star, a star!" "And it's coming to me!"

A glimmer of light,
A small little show,
Whirling around,
Brightening the snow.

It's shining and spinning,
A dance in the clearing.
Giving off bursts of sparkle and glow,
It makes the tree shadows shrink and grow.

An old dappled mouse
Steps forward and bows.
As he points to the star,
He starts speaking out loud.

"Our past, our present, our future–
Each birth, each life, and each death–
In the stars, the story of life is kept."

The star spins near his dear old face,
Then circles his head, all with such grace.

"Although we are missed,
   We're not really gone.
   We're right here still
   And life moves on."

"Like light from the stars,
   We're here and we're there.
   We watch those we love
   With such tender care."

"And we'll meet again,
   This isn't the end.
   We'll see each other
   Once more, my friends."

The star dances up, back the way it came,
Leaving everything all exactly the same.

As the clearing turns light
And the twilight lifts,
It seems as if
The stars do shift.

A brown mouse turns around and does declare,
"Whenever you need us, we're always right there!"
The two curious mice then nod in sync,
And the wise brown mouse gives them a wink.

The animals fade back into the night
As the glowing moon returns to sight.

Then the silver mouse says
To the two, their eyes bright:

"Listen now."

"Departed loved ones you've just seen.
Friends, cousins, sisters, brothers,
Nieces, nephews, fathers and mothers,
Grandmothers, grandfathers, and in-laws too,
Many of whom have always known you."

"They're not truly gone, but watch over you forever;
Always guardian angels, not doubting you ever."

The silver mouse looks back up toward the sky,

And just as he does, a star flies right by.

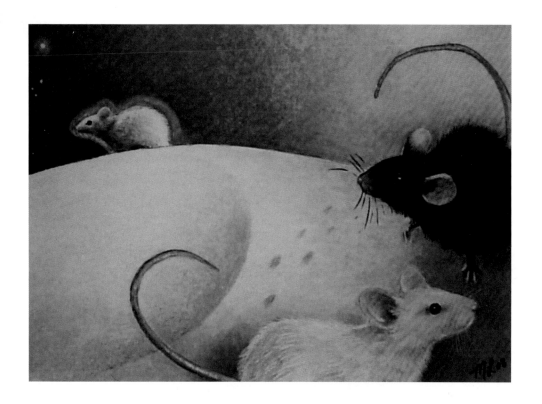

As he moves away from the other two,
He tells them goodnight and bids them adieu.

Now the two mice, with a life lesson learned,
Head home for a rest they know they have earned.

"Remember us!" whispers a voice in their heads.
"I will!" promises each as they crawl into bed.

At home, the two mice then curl up tight.
They'll treasure forever what happened this night.

So, whenever you feel alone or in doubt -
Never fear.

Simply believe -
Know that your loved ones are always ever near.

Visit the author at:

www.moonlightmemoirs.com

Visit the artist at:

www.melodylealamb.com

Maggie Mei Lewis, Melody Lea Lamb and Good Times Press, LLC
join in dedicating a portion of the proceeds from *Moonlight Memoirs*
to projects that provide for the health and safety of animals in need.